STU

ALLEN COUNTY PUBLIC LIBRARY

3 1833 00690 8344

FRIENDS
OF ACPL

D1480416

The Sugar Pear Tree

The Sugar Pear Tree

BY CLYDE ROBERT BULLA

ILLUSTRATED BY TARO YASHIMA

Thomas Y. Crowell Company · New York

Text copyright © 1960 by Clyde Robert Bulla. Illustrations copyright © 1960 by Taro Yashima. All rights reserved. No part of this book may be reproduced in any form, except by a reviewer, without the permission of the publisher. Manufactured in the United States of America. Library of Congress Catalog Card No. 60-5055

1 2 3 4 5 6 7 8 9 10

U! S. 1186682

To the Freemans—
Lydia, Don, and Roy

CONTENTS

The Sugar Pear Tree

CHAPTER 1

"My Favorite Tree"

It was a day in September. Lonnie was on his way home from school.

As he walked along, he looked up at the trees. Some of them were elms. Some were tall palm trees.

There was a bicycle lying on the sidewalk. Lonnie ran into it. He almost fell down.

Someone said, "Watch where you're going!"

He looked around. A boy was coming up the street.

"Oh–hello, Brad," said Lonnie.

Brad was a new boy in school. He had come into Room 6 just three days before.

"I saw you with your head in the air," he said. "I

I

knew you were going to run into something. What were you looking at up there?"

"I was looking at the trees," said Lonnie.

"What for?" asked Brad.

"I don't know which is my favorite tree," said Lonnie. "I'm making up my mind."

"Oh!" said Brad. "Haven't you written that old composition yet?"

"No," said Lonnie. "I don't know which tree to write about."

They walked along together.

"Write about any tree. It doesn't matter," said Brad.

"But the teacher said to write a composition about our *favorite* tree," said Lonnie, "and I don't know which is my favorite."

"My mother helped me," said Brad. "Can't your mother help you?"

"She doesn't have much time," said Lonnie. "She's a nurse, and she goes out to take care of people."

"Get your father to help you," said Brad.

"I don't have any father," said Lonnie.

They came to the street where he lived.

"I'm glad I don't live on this street," said Brad.

"I like it here," said Lonnie.

"That's too bad," said Brad, "because you're going to have to move."

Lonnie said nothing.

"They're going to build a new freeway through here," said Brad. "They're going to take out all the houses to make room for it. Didn't you know that?"

"My great-grandfather says not to believe everything

you hear," said Lonnie. "Do you want to come down and see where I live?"

"What for?" asked Brad.

"We can look at the river," said Lonnie. "My house is close to the river."

Brad laughed. "It's a funny river. There's no water in it."

"There is when it rains," said Lonnie. "And the trains run on the other side of the river. We can see the trains."

"I can see them from my house," said Brad.

Lonnie went on alone. He did not think that he and Brad were going to be friends.

Lonnie lived in the last house on the street. It was a little house with thick, white walls and a low roof.

Once it had been a ranch house, his mother told him. The city had grown and covered the ranch. It had almost taken the house, too. The street went by and took the front yard. Someone had built a wall that cut off the back yard and part of the house. But most of the house was left.

Lonnie went inside. His great-grandfather was sitting by the window.

"I'm home, Gramp," said Lonnie.

"Yes, yes," said his great-grandfather. He was an old, old man. His hair was white. His face was long and thin. "Come here, boy," he said.

Lonnie went to the window. Across the river a train was going by. A man was walking on top of the cars. Sometimes he jumped from one car to another.

"I used to do that," said Gramp. "When I worked on the railroad I did it every day. I could still do it."

"Don't you try it," said Lonnie. "You might fall."

He got out his tablet and pencil. He lay down on the floor.

"What are you doing?" asked Gramp.

"I'm going to write my composition," said Lonnie. "I have to have it tomorrow."

"What composition?" asked Gramp.

"I told you," said Lonnie. "I have to write about my favorite tree. The best composition wins a prize."

"You try hard," said Gramp. "Maybe you can win it."

"I never did win a prize," said Lonnie.

"There's always a first time," said Gramp. "What *is* your favorite tree?"

"I can't make up my mind," said Lonnie.

The old man shut his eyes. Lonnie thought he had gone to sleep. Lonnie wrote, "My Favorite Tree." He tried to think.

The old man spoke. "Do you remember when you

and your mother came back to Tennessee to visit? That was before I came out here to live. You stayed with me, and you were just five years old."

"I remember," said Lonnie.

"There was a tree in my back yard," said Gramp. "I put up a swing for you in that tree. You played out there all by yourself. You used to climb that tree and hang upside down."

"I remember!" said Lonnie. "Gramp, I think *that* tree is my favorite."

He began to write. He was writing when his mother came home.

"You look tired, Mary," said the old man. "Sit down and rest."

"Oh, Grandfather, I can't," she said. "I have to get dinner for you and Lonnie. Then I have to go out to work again." She smiled at Lonnie. "What are you doing?"

"Writing my composition," he said. "It's about my favorite tree."

"What *is* your favorite?" she asked.

"The sugar pear tree," he said.

CHAPTER 2
The Tall Man

In the morning Lonnie took his composition to school. Outside Room 6 he met Brad. Alice and Helen and Phil were there, too. They all looked at Lonnie and laughed.

"Did you get home all right yesterday?" asked Helen.

"We heard you were looking at the trees," said Alice. "We heard you couldn't see where you were going."

"He was walking like this," said Brad. He walked across the hall and ran into the wall. "He was looking for a tree to write about."

"I know who is going to win the prize," said Phil.

"Who?" asked Alice.

"You are," said Phil.

"How do you know?" asked Alice.

"Because you always win the prizes," said Phil.

The bell rang. They went into Room 6. Lonnie gave his composition to the teacher, Miss White.

The teacher told the class, "All the compositions are in now. On Monday we'll know who wins the prize."

"What is the prize going to be?" asked Helen.

"It's a surprise," said the teacher. "Someone will be here to tell you about it."

"I know who is going to win," said Phil, and he looked at Alice.

"We'll all know on Monday," said Miss White.

Lonnie walked home from school alone. His street was quiet. Almost every house was empty. On some of them were red and yellow signs: "House for Sale."

They gave him a strange feeling. He was glad when he came to his house and found no sign on it.

He went inside. A tall man was there, talking with Gramp.

"Wait outside, boy," said Gramp.

Lonnie went out. He sat on the front step. After a while he heard a loud, angry voice, "Get out and stay out!" It was Gramp's voice.

The tall man came out. He said, "I don't want any trouble."

Gramp came to the doorway. "There won't *be* any trouble. Just get out and leave me alone!"

The tall man went away.

Gramp was so angry he was shaking all over. He went back into the house.

Lonnie went with him. "What's the matter?" he asked.

"Nothing," said Gramp.

"Who was that man?" asked Lonnie.

"Never mind," said Gramp. "I'm the head of this family, and I'll take care of things." He sat down. "Your mother works hard. We don't want to worry her, do we?"

"No," said Lonnie.

"Well, then," said Gramp, "we won't tell her what happened."

"I don't *know* what happened," said Lonnie. "Who was that man, and what did he want?"

"We don't have to think about him any more," said Gramp. "He won't be back."

Lonnie's mother came home.

"Is everything all right?" she asked.

"Yes, Mary," said Gramp.

"You are both so quiet," she said. "Are you sure nothing is wrong?"

"Everything is fine," said Gramp. "Everything is just fine."

CHAPTER 3

The Prize

On Monday there was excitement in Room 6. The boys and girls waited. All morning they waited. Still the teacher said nothing about the contest.

In the afternoon a man came to the room. His hair was black and curly. He kept smiling, and his teeth were white.

He sat in a chair by the teacher's desk.

"We have a visitor," said Miss White. "I'm sure some of you know him already. Our visitor's name is Mr. DeJohn."

Lonnie had known him for more than a year. He had a flower shop near the school. Outside the shop he had plants and young trees for sale. On the fence was a sign: "Nick DeJohn—Plant Nursery."

"Mr. DeJohn likes boys and girls, and he likes trees," said Miss White. "When I told him about the compositions you were writing, he wanted to be here today. Later I'll tell you why. Now I know you are waiting for me to talk about the compositions and tell you who won the prize."

Boys and girls began to look at Alice. She turned pink and looked down at her desk.

"There were some very good compositions. It was hard to choose the best," said Miss White, "but the prize goes to—"

"Alice!" whispered Phil.

Miss White shook her head. "The prize goes to Lonnie."

Lonnie sat up straight. He was so surprised he could not think of anything to say.

"I know we would all like to hear Lonnie's composition," said Miss White, "so I am going to ask him to read it to us."

Lonnie went up to Miss White's desk. He took his composition and read it aloud:

"My Favorite Tree"

"When I was five years old I went to Tennessee. I went to see my great-grandfather. He had a tree in his back yard. It was a sugar pear tree, and it is my favorite.

"There was a swing in the tree. My great-grandfather put it up for me. I could swing as high as the house. I liked to climb the tree. It was easy to climb. In the spring it was all in bloom. The flowers were white. They smelled good.

"The tree was so pretty that people came to see it. It was a useful tree, too. It made shade for people. The flowers gave honey to the bees. In the fall there were pears on the tree for my great-grandfather and his friends. The pears were as sweet as sugar.

"For all these reasons, my favorite tree is the sugar pear tree."

Everyone clapped when he was through. "Thank you, Lonnie," said the teacher, as he sat down.

Then Nick spoke to the class. He said, "Your teacher told me you were writing about trees. I asked her, 'Will you make it a contest and let me give a prize?' Now Lonnie has won, and I will tell you what the prize is. It is a tree from my nursery. Stop after school, Lonnie, and I'll help you choose your tree."

Nick said good-by and went away.

"It will be wonderful to have a tree of your own and watch it grow," said Miss White.

"Yes!" said Lonnie. He thought of his mother and Gramp—how proud they would be when he told them he had won the prize.

After school he went to the flower shop.

"Come into my yard and look at the trees," said Nick.

In the yard were dozens of trees. There were palms and elms and pines. There were oranges and lemons. Some grew in big wooden boxes. Some grew in small round cans.

"These little trees are one or two years old," said

Nick. "The bigger ones are older. Do you see any you like?"

Lonnie walked among the trees. "I like them all. I don't know which to choose." He asked, "Do you have a pear tree?"

"Yes, I do," said Nick. "I have one left."

He showed the tree to Lonnie. It was two years old. It was a straight little tree, three feet high, and it had six branches.

"Is it a sugar pear tree?" asked Lonnie.

"Yes, you could call it a sugar pear tree," said Nick. "Some day it will have pears that are little and round and sweet. Is this the one you'd like to have?"

Lonnie looked about him. Of all the trees in the yard, he liked the pear tree best. "Yes," he said, "this is the one."

"Where do you live?" asked Nick.

"By the river," said Lonnie.

"I'll put the tree in my truck and take it home for you," said Nick.

"Thank you," said Lonnie, "but I can carry it."

"It's pretty heavy," said Nick. "This can of dirt is the heavy part."

He set the tree in the back of his truck. Lonnie rode in front and told Nick which way to go.

They stopped at Lonnie's house. Lonnie's mother had just come home.

"Mother, I won!" he said. "My composition was the best, and I won the prize!"

"Oh, Lonnie," she said, "I'm so proud of you!"

"This is Nick," said Lonnie. "He gave me my prize. It's a pear tree, mother."

Nick got out of the truck and took off his hat.

"How do you do?" said Lonnie's mother. "Don't you remember me, Mr. DeJohn?"

"Yes, I do. You've been to my flower shop," said Nick. "But I didn't know you were Lonnie's mother."

"It was kind of you to give him the prize," she said.

"I was glad to," said Nick.

He drove away.

Lonnie's mother looked at the tree on the door step. Gramp came out to see it.

"I won it," said Lonnie. "It's a sugar pear tree."

"That's fine, boy," said Gramp.

"Yes, it's fine, only– Oh, dear!" said Lonnie's mother.

All at once Lonnie knew why she had said, "Oh, dear!" The house had no front yard. It had no back yard. It had no yard on either side. There was nowhere to plant the sugar pear tree.

CHAPTER 4

At the Beach

"Don't worry, boy." That was what Gramp kept saying. "We'll find a place for your tree."

But time went by until September was almost gone. Still they had found nowhere to plant the tree.

They talked about it one night.

"Maybe we could plant the tree in front of the house," said Gramp. "I could take up a piece of the sidewalk to make room for it."

"You couldn't do that," said Lonnie's mother. "Besides, we don't want to plant the tree here. One of these days everything on this street will have to go."

"Why will it?" asked Gramp.

"To make room for the freeway," she said. "You know that."

"No, I *don't* know it!" said Gramp. "They'd better not try to take our house."

"Grandfather, please don't talk that way," she said. "This house is not ours. We only rent it from the state. When the state tells us to go, we'll have to go."

"Oh, no, we won't," said Gramp. "They can't push us around."

Lonnie went outside. There on the front step was his tree in its round can of dirt. He put his hands on the small, smooth trunk. It felt cool and alive.

He was sitting there when Nick drove up.

"Hello, Lonnie." Nick got out of the truck. "How is your tree?"

"All right," said Lonnie.

"It should be planted," said Nick. "That can will soon be too small for the roots."

Lonnie's mother came to the door. She smiled when she saw Nick.

Nick took off his hat. "I'd like to ask you something. Tomorrow is Sunday, you know—"

She laughed. "Yes, I know tomorrow is Sunday."

"Well," said Nick, "if it's a nice day, would you and your family like to go somewhere with me? Would you like to go to the beach?"

Lonnie looked at his mother. "We haven't been to the beach for a long time."

"I'm all alone," said Nick. "I get lonesome on Sundays. If you go with me, I won't get lonesome."

"All right," said Lonnie's mother.

Sunday was a fine day. Nick came early to take them to the beach.

Lonnie took his tree into the house.

"Why don't you leave it outside?" asked his mother.

"Something might happen to it while I'm gone," he said.

They drove to the beach. Nick parked close to the ocean. The wind blew into the truck, and the air was fresh and clean.

Lonnie ran down to the edge of the water. He dug in the sand. He picked up shells.

Gramp went to sleep under a big umbrella. Nick and Lonnie's mother walked together. Part of the time Lonnie walked with them. Part of the time he played with a boy and girl who had brought their dog to the beach.

The dog liked to play in the water. He always shook himself when he came out. He shook water all over them.

The boy asked Lonnie, "Do you have a dog at home?"

"No," said Lonnie.

"Do you have a cat or a bird?" asked the girl.

"No," said Lonnie, "but I have a tree."

His mother called him. She and Gramp and Nick were under the big umbrella. Nick had bought four ice-cream cones. They sat on the sand and ate them. Then it was time to go home.

"It's nice at the beach," said Gramp, "but I'm glad to get home."

"I had a good time," said Lonnie.

"So did I," said his mother.

They stopped outside the house.

"I'm going to bring my tree out into the fresh air now," said Lonnie.

His mother said to Nick, "He talks as if his tree were another person."

"I think it *is* like another person to him," said Nick. "I know how he feels. Sometimes a tree is like a person to me, too."

CHAPTER 5
A Good Home

The next day Lonnie walked part of the way home from school with Brad. They came to Lonnie's street, and Brad pointed.

"Look," he said.

The whole street looked strange. In a moment Lonnie knew why. Two of the houses were off the ground. There were wheels underneath them. There were fifteen or twenty wheels under each house.

"I told you," said Brad. "They're getting ready to move out all the houses."

Lonnie ran home.

At the door he stopped. The houses on wheels were

forgotten. That morning he had left his tree on the front step. Now it was gone.

He ran into the house. "Gramp!" he shouted. "Where is my tree?"

Gramp was sitting by the window. "Hold your horses, boy," he said.

"Where is it?" Lonnie looked about him. "Did you bring it inside?"

"Sit down and cool off," said Gramp. "I told you I'd find a place for your tree, and today I found one. You remember Charlie Norris?"

Lonnie remembered him. Mr. Norris was an old man, almost as old as Gramp. He lived a few blocks away, and he and Gramp were friends.

"Charlie came by and saw your tree," said Gramp. "He has trees in his yard, but he didn't have a pear tree. He wanted to take it off your hands."

"Did you give him my tree?" cried Lonnie.

"I thought you'd be glad," said Gramp. "I found a good home for your tree. Charlie Norris has just the place for it."

"That was my tree," said Lonnie. "You didn't have any right to give it away."

"What were you going to do with it?" said Gramp. "Let it sit there and dry up?"

Lonnie said again, "That was *my* tree!"

He ran out the door. He ran all the way to Charlie Norris' house.

He knocked at the door, and no one answered.

He went around to the back yard. Mr. Norris was there. He was sitting in a chair, smoking his pipe.

"Mr. Norris!" said Lonnie.

"What say?" asked the old man.

"I want my tree," said Lonnie.

"What?" asked the old man.

"My tree!" said Lonnie.

"Your tree? It's a nice one," said the old man. "I'm going to plant it right there by the fence."

"No!" said Lonnie. "It's mine."

The old man put his hand to his ear. "What say?"

"It's mine!" shouted Lonnie. "What did you do with it?"

Then he saw the pear tree behind Mr. Norris' chair. It was still in its can of dirt.

Lonnie ran to the tree. He picked it up.

"What are you doing?" cried the old man. "Come back here!"

Lonnie did not stop. He carried the tree away. He carried it home and put it back on the step.

Gramp came out of the house. "What's the matter with you?" he said. "Charlie Norris was going to give your tree a good home."

"Don't you ever give my tree away again," said Lonnie.

"Don't be telling me what to do, boy," said Gramp. "I'm head of this family, and don't you forget it."

Lonnie said nothing. He sat there with his arm around the tree. And, as he looked up the street, one of the houses on wheels began to move. Slowly it swung out into the street. A truck was pulling it away.

CHAPTER 6
A Scrap of Paper

A few days later, on his way home from school, Lonnie stopped at Nick's shop. He went into the yard beside the shop. He looked at the new trees and the flat boxes of little plants.

Nick came out into the yard.

"See my new plants, Lonnie?" he said. "I brought them from the valley this morning."

"Is that where you live?" asked Lonnie.

"I don't have much of a home," said Nick. "Two men work on my farm in the valley. Sometimes I stay with them, and sometimes I sleep here in the back of my shop. What can I do for you today? How is your tree?"

30

"That's what I wanted to ask you about," said Lonnie. "One of the leaves is yellow. Does that mean something is wrong?"

"It was a good, strong tree when I gave it to you," said Nick.

"Do you—do you think my tree is going to die?" asked Lonnie.

"No, I don't think so," said Nick, "but don't forget to water it, and try to get it planted as soon as you can."

Lonnie walked slowly home. There were more empty places on his street where houses had been taken away. The places were ugly, as if the houses had been dug out of the ground. He tried not to look at them.

At the end of the street he saw something strange. Gramp was out on the sidewalk with a pail of water in one hand and a brush in the other. He was washing the front of the house!

"What are you doing?" asked Lonnie.

The old man jumped and dropped the brush.

"Get on in the house," he said in a cross voice, "and don't be asking questions."

When Lonnie's mother came home, she said, "There's a spot on the front of the house. It looks wet."

"I washed off the front," said Gramp. "It looks better, doesn't it?"

"Yes," she said," but don't do too much work on the house. I know we can't stay here much longer."

"We can stay here as long as we want to," said Gramp.

"Oh, no," she said. "I think we are the only ones left on the street. I don't know why they've let us stay this long."

They had dinner. Then it was time for Lonnie's mother to go back to work. Lonnie walked with her to the corner. He waited with her until her bus came.

When he went home, it was still daylight. On the front of the house he saw a red and yellow scrap of paper. He pulled at it, and it came off in his hand.

The signs on the other houses along the street were red and yellow. Now he knew why Gramp had been washing the house.

He went inside. "Gramp—" he said.

The old man was sitting by the window. "What do you want, boy?" he asked.

"I found this on the house." Lonnie held out the scrap of paper.

"Well?" said Gramp.

"I know what it is," said Lonnie. "Somebody put a sign on this house. It means our house is for sale to be moved—just like the others. And you washed it off."

"What if I did?" said Gramp.

"This house doesn't belong to us," said Lonnie. "They can put us out."

"I'd like to see them try it." Gramp took the scrap of paper and put it in his pocket. "Don't say anything about this to your mother."

"I have to tell her," said Lonnie.

"No, you don't," said Gramp. "It would just worry her. Why do you think I pay the rent and go to the grocery store and do so many things around the place? Because I want to save her all the work and worry I can."

"But when she finds out—" said Lonnie.

"You don't want to worry her, do you? She likes this house, boy, and so do I. We just wouldn't feel at home anywhere else. You want to stay here, don't you?"

"Yes," said Lonnie, "but—"

"Then you leave everything to me," said Gramp. "They can build their old freeway without taking this house. I looked at a map, and I know."

Lonnie went to bed. He lay awake in the dark. He heard his mother come home. He thought, I'll get up and tell her.

Then he thought, No, she's tired now. I'll wait till morning.

In the morning, she called him. "I'm taking care of a little sick girl, and I have to go to work early. Gramp will get your breakfast. Your school lunch is in the bag on the table. Good-by."

She was gone before he remembered what it was he had to tell her.

U! S. 1186682

CHAPTER 7

That Evening

Gramp said that evening, "Your mother is working late again tonight, boy. I'll get supper. What do you want to eat?"

Gramp was not a very good cook. He could make pancakes better than anything else.

"I'd like pancakes," said Lonnie.

Gramp made a stack of pancakes. He and Lonnie ate their supper together.

Lonnie said, "I've been thinking. I have to tell mother about the house."

"Now don't start that," said Gramp. "You don't have to tell her anything."

"But it's for sale and she doesn't know it," said Lonnie. "Somebody has to tell her."

"Don't you worry your head," said Gramp. "We're going to stay right here. They can't move this house away as long as we're in it."

They went into the front room. It was growing dark. Gramp pulled the shades.

Lonnie heard a car stop outside.

"Maybe it's Nick," he said.

He opened the door. Outside stood a policeman. Behind him was another policeman. Out in the street were two big men in overalls.

Gramp came to the door. The first policeman had a paper in his hand. He gave it to Gramp. The old man looked at it and threw it on the floor. He tried to shut the door.

But the policeman had his foot in the doorway. He came on into the room. "Let's not have any trouble," he said.

"There won't *be* any trouble," said Gramp, "if you get out and leave us alone."

"Listen to me," said the policeman. "This house be-
longs to the state. It has to be taken out because the freeway is coming through here. You were told to move. You
were told three times. As long as you won't go, we're
going to have to move you out."

"You can't do it!" said Gramp.

The two men in overalls came in. The other policeman
came with them. They began to carry things out of the
house.

Gramp shook his fist. He shouted at the men. They
hardly looked at him.

At last he sat down in his chair by the window. "All right!" he said. "*Take* everything out of the house, but you won't get me out of this chair!"

The men worked very fast. In a little while the house was empty. Only Gramp's chair was left.

The two policemen looked at each other. They picked up the chair, one on each side. They carried it out, with Gramp still sitting in it. They set it down on the sidewalk.

They nailed the door and windows shut. They put a lock on the door.

One of the policemen said to Lonnie, "Do you have a place to stay tonight? Can we take you anywhere?"

"No," said Lonnie. "We have to wait here for my mother."

"We're sorry about this," said the policeman, "but it had to be done."

The men drove away. Lonnie and Gramp were alone. Gramp had not moved from his chair. The street light shone down on his head. He put his hands over his face and began to cry.

Lonnie remembered his tree. He looked on the front step.

"Gramp!" he cried. "My tree is gone!"

He began to look among the pieces of furniture. Under a table he found the tree. It had been pushed off the step. The men had set the table down over it.

The tree was bent far to one side. At first he thought it was broken, but when he moved the table, the tree stood straight again.

He saw his mother coming down the street. He went to meet her.

"Lonnie! What on earth—!" she said.

"The police were here," he told her. "They moved us out."

"Oh, Grandfather!" she said. "I thought you were taking care of things here at home."

Gramp did not look at her. He sat there with his hands over his face.

Lonnie said to his mother, "Wait. I'll be right back."

He picked up his tree and carried it away.

CHAPTER 8
The Greenhouse

The tree in its can of dirt was heavy. At the end of the street Lonnie set it down. He rested for a minute or two before he picked it up and went on.

He came to Nick's shop. The front of it was dark. The yard beside it was dark, too. The gate was shut, but it was not locked.

Lonnie went into the yard. He put the tree down with the others that were there. He looked at it for a little while. He started away.

Someone called out, "Who's there?"

There was a light in the back of the shop. Someone came out into the yard. It was Nick.

42

"Who's there?" he asked again. "Lonnie, is that you?"

"Yes," said Lonnie.

"What are you doing?" asked Nick. "Did you want to see me?"

"I brought back the tree," said Lonnie.

"The pear tree?" asked Nick. "What for?"

"I don't have any place for it," said Lonnie. "Maybe I'll *never* have a place. I can't take care of it. And we'll be moving around now. Something might happen to it. So I brought it back."

"What do you mean?" asked Nick. "Why will you be moving around? Where are you going?"

"I don't know," said Lonnie. "They put us out of the house. I don't know where we'll go."

He said good-by to Nick. He went back to where he had left his mother and Gramp. Gramp was still in his chair. Mother was sitting near him.

"Where have you been, Lonnie?" she asked, but she did not wait for him to answer. "I'm trying to think what to do. Nothing like this ever happened to me before."

"It isn't cold," he said. "Can we sleep out here tonight?"

She shook her head. "We could go to a hotel. But I don't like to go away and leave all our things here."

A car came down the street and stopped. It was Nick's truck. Nick got out.

"How did this happen?" he asked. "How could such a thing happen?"

Mother went to meet him. She said, "Grandfather didn't tell us we had to move, and the police put us out. He's so old and he gets strange ideas, and now—Nick," she said in a whisper, "there's something wrong. He just sits there. He doesn't say a word."

Nick went to the old man. He tried to talk to him. Mother tried, too.

"I don't blame you, Grandfather," she said. "I blame myself. I thought I had to be so busy all the time. I was so busy I couldn't look after my home and my family."

Gramp looked straight ahead and said nothing.

Mother looked at Nick. "What am I going to do?" she said.

"I'll take you with me," he said. "I know a place where you can sleep tonight."

He and Lonnie put some of the clothing and furniture into the truck.

"I'll get the rest later," said Nick. He led Gramp to the truck. The old man drew back.

"Come on," said Nick. "We're all going."

Then Gramp got into the seat with the others.

They drove away. They left the lights and the noise of the city behind them.

It was more than an hour before they came to Nick's farm. Lonnie saw a small, dark house.

"Are we going to stay here?" he asked.

"No," said Nick. "This is where my two men sleep. I'll put you in my greenhouse."

"What is a greenhouse?" asked Lonnie.

"It's the glass house where I grow plants." Nick drove a little farther and stopped. "Here it is."

The greenhouse was big and square. The walls and roof were made of glass.

They went into the room in the front of the greenhouse. Nick turned on a light.

"This was an office," he said. "It hasn't been used for a long time, and I'm afraid it's pretty dusty. Do you think you can sleep here?"

"Yes," said Lonnie's mother.

Nick and Lonnie took the beds out of the truck and set them up in the office.

Mother said, "We'll be sleeping in our own beds tonight after all. I don't know how we can ever thank Nick for helping us so much.''

Lonnie went to bed. The air in the greenhouse was warm and damp. It smelled like the woods after a summer rain. He lay there and looked out through the glass front of the office. The moon was shining through the window. That was the last thing he saw before he went to sleep.

CHAPTER 9

A Pretty Sight

Lonnie's mother said, "I don't want you to miss school."

There was a school not far from Nick's farm.

"I'm going to send you there," she said.

Lonnie did not want to go to the school. "I won't know anybody there," he said. "Can't I wait till we go back to the city?"

"I don't know when that will be," she said. "I can't go look for a place to live just now. I have to stay with Grandfather."

"But won't I have to tell the old school I'm going to a new school?" asked Lonnie.

"Yes," she said. "Maybe you can ride to the city with Nick tomorrow. I'll write a letter for you to take to your teacher."

So the next day Lonnie rode to the city in Nick's truck. He went to school and gave his mother's letter to Miss White.

The teacher was glad to see him. "I didn't know where you'd gone," she said. "I'm so glad you're all right, but we'll be sorry to lose you, Lonnie."

The boys and girls were glad to see him, too.

"When you stopped coming to school," said Phil, "I went to your house to look for you."

"I went to your house, too," said Brad. "I went twice. We didn't know where you'd gone."

Lonnie stayed at school all day. They gave a party for him in Room 6 because he was going away. They played games and sang songs. Every boy and girl in the room drew a picture for Lonnie.

"These are for you to keep," said Miss White. "Then you won't forget us. Come to see us whenever you can."

"I will, thank you," said Lonnie.

That evening he rode back to the farm with Nick. He was quiet all the way. He was sorry to leave his old school.

In the morning he went to the new school. It was smaller than the school in the city. He looked about him at the strange faces. He told himself, I don't want to go to this school.

And after the first day he found he liked it there. He liked being the new boy. The other boys and girls wanted to sit with him in the lunchroom. They asked him about school in the city. They taught him games he had never played before.

But he always felt sad when he went back to the greenhouse. It was not really a home. The office was too small for all their furniture. There was no place for a stove. When his mother cooked, she had to go up the road to the farmhouse. Most of the time she looked as if she had been crying. Gramp stayed in bed all day.

Nick brought a doctor to see him.

"I can hardly get him to eat," Lonnie's mother told the doctor, "and he won't speak to anyone. He hasn't said a word since we came here."

"What happened in the city was a shock to him," said the doctor.

"Yes, it was a shock," she said. "He liked the little house. It was home to him."

"There isn't much I can do," said the doctor, "unless he *wants* to get well."

Lonnie's mother told Nick what the doctor had said. Nick thought for a while. "I have a plan," he said. "It might help him get well."

He told her his plan.

"Oh, no," she said. "You've already done so much. We can't let you do *that!*"

"I *want* to do it," said Nick. "It might be a good thing for us all."

And one day, when Lonnie came home from school, he saw a house beside the greenhouse. It was a small, white house with wheels under it.

Mother and Nick were there, looking at it.

"What did Gramp say?" asked Lonnie.

"Nothing," said his mother. There were tears in her eyes. "I tried to talk to him. He wouldn't listen."

Lonnie ran into the greenhouse. Gramp was in bed, with his face turned away.

"See what's outside," said Lonnie.

The old man opened one eye and shut it again.

"You've got to look!" Lonnie pulled Gramp up in bed and turned his head so that he had to look out.

The old man sat there, looking out through the window.

"See, Gramp?" said Lonnie. "It's our house—where we lived in the city. Nick got it for us. He likes my mother, Gramp, and he likes us, too, so he got our house and had it moved out here. We're going to live in it, and you can sit by the window and look at the— Well, maybe

there won't be trains, but you can see the cars go by."

Mother called him. He went outside.

"Here's something for you," she said.

Nick had taken something out of his truck. It was a little tree in a can of dirt.

"It's my tree!" said Lonnie. "I mean, it *was* mine."

"It's still yours," said Nick. "I was just keeping it until you had a place for it."

Lonnie went to the tree. He touched it. "It has new leaves here in the top," he said. "Look at the new leaves."

The door of the greenhouse opened. Gramp came out, walking very slowly. He had put on his clothes. He stood and looked at the house.

"Yes, yes!" he said.

"See my tree?" said Lonnie. "Nick brought it to me. Will you help me plant it?"

"I'll help you, boy," said Gramp.

"Shall I plant it in the front yard or the back?" asked Lonnie.

"In the front," said Gramp. "Plant it here in the front where everybody can see it. A sugar pear tree is a pretty sight."

About the Author

CLYDE ROBERT BULLA composes music and writes stories for children at his home in Los Angeles, California. Born near King City, Missouri, he began his formal education in a little one-room schoolhouse. It was here that he wrote his first stories and composed his first songs. After graduation from high school, Mr. Bulla sold several short stories and then wrote his first book. Meanwhile, he worked on a local newspaper as a columnist and linotype operator.

His books for children met with great success, and after a time he gave up his newspaper work and devoted all his time to writing and composing. Mr. Bulla's interest in travel has taken him to Europe, Hawaii, Mexico, and to many cities throughout the United States.

About the Artist

TARO YASHIMA has illustrated several books for children, although this is his first in collaboration with his personal friend and art student, Clyde Robert Bulla. Born in Kagoshima, Japan, Mr. Yashima studied at the Imperial Art Academy of Tokyo. In 1939 he came to the United States and studied further at the Art Students League in New York City. Mr. Yashima is a member of several societies for artists in this country, and his works have been shown with many public and private collections. He is, as well, a collector of early American folk art. His home is in Los Angeles, California, where Mr. Yashima and his wife are instructors of art at the Japanese-American Art Institute, which they have established.